# The Trouble with Darwin

# Discovery Facts

**Chimpanzees:** Chimps can be found living in the forests of twenty-one African countries. They are omnivores, and like humans, they have opposable thumbs, use tools, laugh, and play.

One hundred years ago as many as two million chimps lived in the forests of Africa. Now experts estimate there are no more than 150,000 left living in the wild. Chimpanzees are disappearing as their forest homes are destroyed, as they are hunted for meat, and as poachers kill mother chimps and sell their babies as pets.

**Dr. Jane Goodall:** The doctor has been studying chimpanzees for more than forty years. By patiently watching the chimpanzees in their natural habitat, Dr. Goodall discovered that chimps are very similar to humans. Over the years Dr. Goodall has helped to found environmental conservation groups around the world. Roots & Shoots is the Jane Goodall Institute's environmental and humanitarian program for young people. Dr. Goodall founded Roots & Shoots in 1991 with local students in Tanzania. The program has now grown to more than 3,000 groups in 67 countries. As a member of Roots & Shoots, you can join young people worldwide in making a difference for animals, the environment, and our human community.

If you would like to get involved with Roots & Shoots, please contact:
roots-shoots@janegoodall.org or visit the
Jane Goodall Institute Web site at www.janegoodall.org

Based on the TV series *The Wild Thornberrys* created by Klasky Csupo, Inc. as seen on Nickelodeon

POCKET
BOOKS
First published in Great Britain in 2003 by Pocket Books, an imprint of Simon & Schuster UK Ltd
Africa House, 64-78 Kingsway, London WC2B 6AH

Originally published in 2001 by Simon Spotlight, an imprint of Simon & Schuster Children's Division, New York
© 2003 Viacom International Inc. All rights reserved.
NICKELODEON, *The Wild Thornberrys*, and all related titles, logos and characters are trademarks of Viacom International Inc. Created by Klasky Csupo, Inc.

ISBN 0-743-41547-7

1 3 5 7 9 10 8 6 4 2

# The Trouble with Darwin

by Kiki Thorpe

based on the story by David Regal; teleplay written by Jill Gorey and Barbara Herndon;
and storyboards by Jennifer Coyle, Robert Goodin, Jason Park, and Sean Pendergrass

illustrated by Jim Durk

Pocket Books/Nickelodeon

London          New York          Sydney

"Move it, wildebeest!" Eliza Thornberry yelled. "We're in a hurry!"

Slowly the herd of wildebeest began to move. The Thornberrys had come to Tanzania to film the opening of a chimpanzee sanctuary.

"Are we almost there?" Eliza asked anxiously. She was going to meet the famous chimpanzee researcher Dr. Jane Goodall.

Eliza had been reading about Dr. Goodall, and
knew they had a lot in common.
"When we meet we're gonna be like two old
friends!" she told Darwin.

At last the Thornberrys arrived at the chimp sanctuary.

"This looks like a wonderful place for the orphaned chimps," Marianne said.

"What do you mean *orphaned*?" Debbie asked.

"Poachers often kill the mother chimps to capture their babies and sell them," the sanctuary worker explained.

"Baby chimps can't survive without their mothers. They're helpless," Marianne added.

"Poor little hairy things," Debbie said.

"Debbie, you've done a good job watching Donnie. Why don't you take a break?" Marianne suggested.

"Yes, go and enjoy yourself," Nigel agreed. "I've rigged up something to keep Donnie busy." He pushed a button. Suddenly a giant play set sprang from the side of the Commvee.

"I'm outta here," Debbie said. "Which way to the gift shop?"

"We don't have one," another sanctuary worker replied. "But the education centre is over there."

Debbie shrugged. "Later!" she called to her family.

Meanwhile Eliza had spotted Dr. Goodall and rushed over to meet her.

"Wow! Hi, Dr. Goodall!" she exclaimed. "I'm Eliza Thornberry and you're my biggest fan! I mean – "

"It's nice to meet you, Eliza," Dr. Goodall said.

"We have *so* much in common," Eliza said. "Most of all, we both love chimps! Dr. Goodall, I'd like you to meet Darwin."

Dr. Goodall greeted Darwin by hooting like a chimp. Darwin paused, then hooted back shyly.

"He's not very responsive," said Dr. Goodall. "Would you like a banana, Darwin?"

Darwin wrinkled his nose.

"He's too old to be an orphaned chimp from here," Dr. Goodall noted.

"Darwin lives with me!" Eliza explained. "He's my *best* friend."

Dr. Goodall frowned. "Eliza, chimpanzees are meant to live in the wild. It's not right to turn one into a pet," she said gently.
"But Darwin's *not* like other chimps – ," Eliza started to explain.
"Dr. Goodall! What a pleasure to meet you!" Marianne exclaimed, walking up with Nigel.

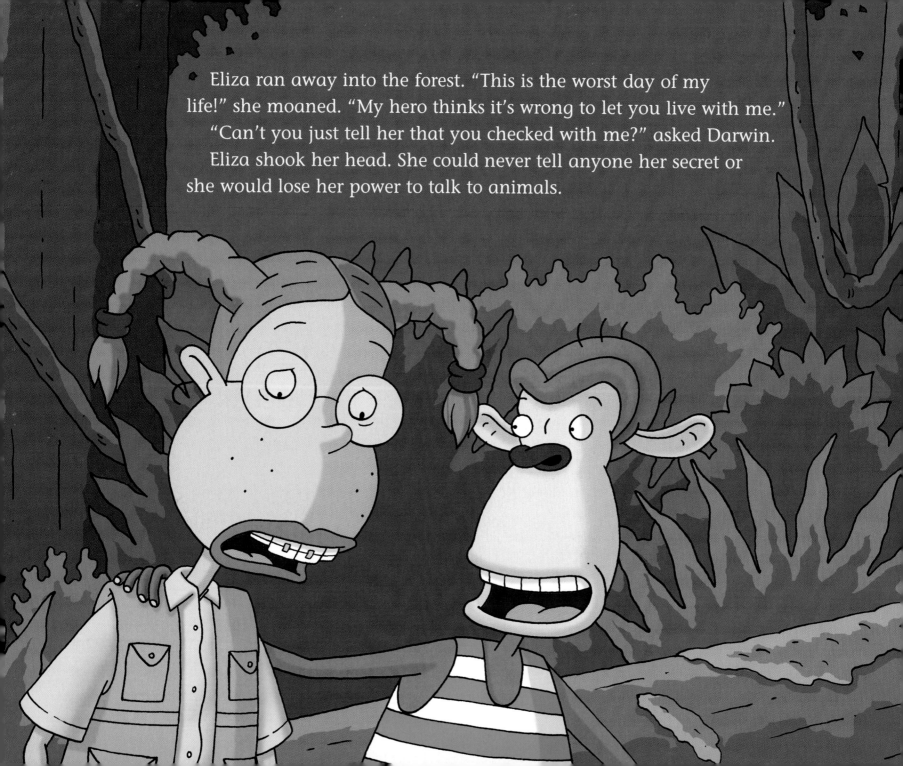

Eliza ran away into the forest. "This is the worst day of my life!" she moaned. "My hero thinks it's wrong to let you live with me."

"Can't you just tell her that you checked with me?" asked Darwin.

Eliza shook her head. She could never tell anyone her secret or she would lose her power to talk to animals.

"It's not the end of the world," Darwin told Eliza.

"It is to me," Eliza responded sadly.

Suddenly a wild hog dashed out from the bushes and ran into Darwin.

"Hey, what's the big idea?" Darwin asked.

"They're here! Get out while you can!" the wild hog grunted. Then he sprinted away.

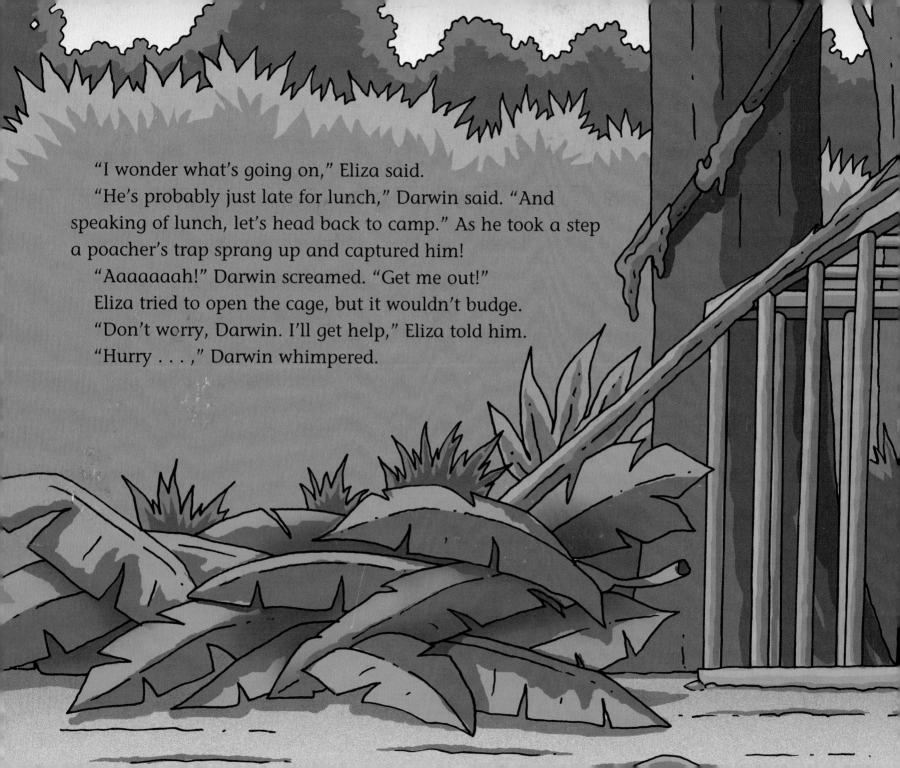

"I wonder what's going on," Eliza said.

"He's probably just late for lunch," Darwin said. "And speaking of lunch, let's head back to camp." As he took a step a poacher's trap sprang up and captured him!

"Aaaaaaah!" Darwin screamed. "Get me out!"

Eliza tried to open the cage, but it wouldn't budge.

"Don't worry, Darwin. I'll get help," Eliza told him.

"Hurry . . . ," Darwin whimpered.

Eliza ran as fast as she could. Near the edge of the forest she heard the rumble of an engine. She peeped around a bush and saw a suspicious-looking truck driving towards Darwin!

There was no time to get help now. Eliza raced back into the forest. "Hang in there, Darwin!" she called. "I'm coming."

Eliza watched helplessly from a hiding spot as two poachers loaded Darwin into the back of their truck.

Suddenly Eliza had an idea.

Eliza crept around to the front of the truck. She saw a shortwave radio and crawled into the cab.

"Hello, is anybody there?" she asked urgently into the radio. "This is an emergency! Poachers are near the sanctuary! They're parked under a baobab tree by the river. Please come – "

Without warning the radio went dead. Eliza looked up.
"What are you doing here?" the poachers grunted.
Then they covered Eliza's mouth, tied her hands and feet with rope,
and shut her in the truck with the captured animals.

Fortunately Dr. Goodall's radio had picked up the signal from Eliza.

"Poachers!" Dr. Goodall gasped. "We've got to be quick!"

"Let's take the Commvee!" cried Nigel.

"Tell security to meet us under the baobab tree by the riverbank," Dr. Goodall instructed a sanctuary worker.

They raced into the forest at top speed.
"There they are!" Dr. Goodall cried when she spotted the
poachers' truck.

Marianne parked the Commvee behind some bushes so they wouldn't be seen.

"Perhaps it would be best to wait for security to get here," Nigel suggested.

"There's no time," Dr. Goodall said.

"What are you going to do when you find the poachers?" Nigel asked.

"I'm not sure . . . wish me luck!" answered Dr. Goodall.

Meanwhile Eliza didn't stay tied up for long. A bushpig chewed through the ropes and set her free.

"I'll be back," she promised the animals.

"What are you going to do?" Darwin asked.

"I'm not sure," she answered. "Wish me luck!"

Eliza hid behind a tree and waited for her chance. As soon as the poachers climbed into their truck, she darted out and began to let the air out of a front tire.

Both Eliza and Dr. Goodall let the air out of the back tires and crept around the truck.

"Eliza! What are you doing here?" Dr. Goodall asked.

"The poachers took Darwin. I had to stop them, so I'm . . . letting the air out of their tires," Eliza answered.

"Great minds think alike," Dr. Goodall said. "Let's go."

"You're not going anywhere," yelled the poachers as they grabbed Eliza and Dr. Goodall.

Suddenly they heard the sound of a trumpeting elephant and saw the Commvee barreling towards them.

"Your poaching days are over!" Nigel shouted as he honked the Commvee's elephantlike horn.

Eliza ran to the truck and let Darwin out of his cage.

"Thank you, thank you!" Darwin exclaimed.

"Oh, Darwin, I don't know what I'd do if anything ever happened to you," said Eliza.

Dr. Goodall smiled as she watched Eliza and Darwin hug each other.

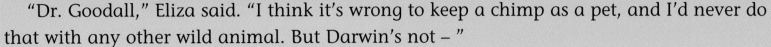

"Dr. Goodall," Eliza said. "I think it's wrong to keep a chimp as a pet, and I'd never do that with any other wild animal. But Darwin's not – "

"Like other animals," Dr. Goodall finished for her. "I know. You two have an almost . . . *magical* . . . relationship. I'll make a deal with you. Keep Darwin, but help spread the word about chimps in captivity. Deal?"

"Deal!" Eliza agreed.

Later Eliza and Darwin sat in the Commvee eating ice-cream sundaes.

"I'm so happy you're staying with me," Eliza told Darwin. "It's almost like Dr. Goodall knows my secret."

"Well, it's no secret that I belong here," Darwin said, smiling at Eliza, "where there's ice cream and hot fudge . . . and my best friend."

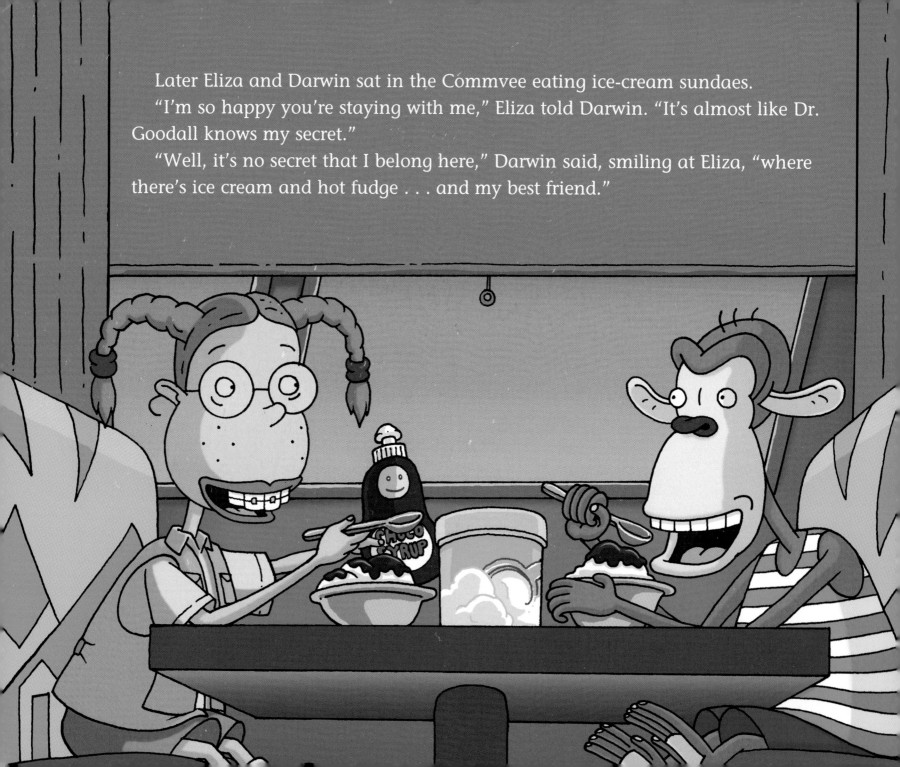